MY FIRST 5 MINUTES FAIRY TALES

★

THE LITTLE MERMAID

Wonder House

Once upon a time, far out in the sea, there lived a Sea King with his Queen and four beautiful daughters.

The youngest princess was the loveliest
and had the most melodious voice.

She was called the Little Mermaid.

On a stormy day, the Little Mermaid was frolicking about when she saw a Prince fall off a ship! She rescued him from drowning and dragged him to the shore.

She looked at him and thought, "Oh! How handsome he is!" The Little Mermaid fell in love with the Prince.

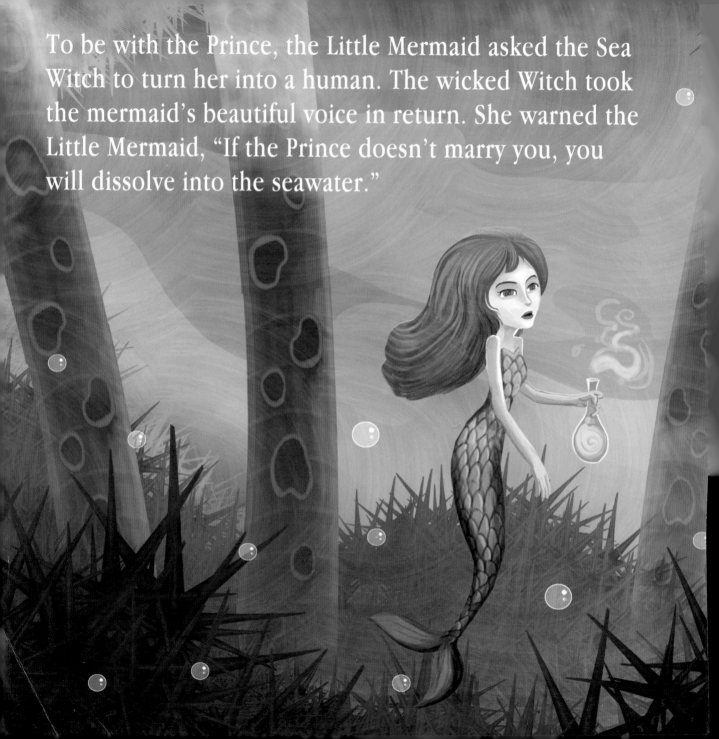

To be with the Prince, the Little Mermaid asked the Sea Witch to turn her into a human. The wicked Witch took the mermaid's beautiful voice in return. She warned the Little Mermaid, "If the Prince doesn't marry you, you will dissolve into the seawater."

The Little Mermaid
agreed and drank the
magic potion.

The Little Mermaid wandered on land until she reached the palace.

"Miss, are you okay?" came a voice. It was the Prince! But the poor girl couldn't reply back, for now she was dumb.

"Let me help you," said the kind Prince. Soon, they became good friends. But the Prince had no idea that the Little Mermaid was his savior.

A few days later, the Prince met a beautiful
Princess. Mistaking her for the girl who
had saved him, the Prince proposed to the
Princess. She said yes!

The Little Mermaid was heartbroken.

The Little Mermaid went to the shore and met her sisters. She told them the entire tale, and her sisters promised to return with a solution.

A while later, her oldest sister returned to the shore with a knife. "I got it from the Sea Witch. If you kill the Prince with this knife, you will become a mermaid again," she said.

That night, the Little Mermaid crept into the Prince's room. But seeing his lovely face she couldn't kill him; she loved him too much. "Goodbye," she whispered, crying.

The air fairies were impressed with Little Mermaid's noble deed. Before she could die, they turned her into an air fairy, and she lived out the rest of her days as Little Fairy!